D1146551

Dear Parents,

Congratulations! Your child has embarked on an exciting journey – they're learning to read! As a parent, you can be there to support and cheer them along as they take their first steps.

At school, children are taught how to decode words and arrange these building blocks of language into sentences and wonderful stories.

At home, parents play a vital part in reinforcing these new-found skills. You can help your child practise their reading by providing well-written, engaging stories, which you can enjoy together.

This series offers exactly that, and more. These stories support inexperienced readers by:

- gradually introducing new vocabulary
- using repetition to consolidate learning
- gradually increasing sentence length and word count
- providing texts that boost a young reader's confidence.

As each book is completed, engaging activities encourage young readers to look back at the story, while a Picture Dictionary reinforces new vocabulary. Enjoyment is the key – and reading together can be great fun for both parent and child!

Prue Goodwin
Lecturer in Literacy and Children's Books

How to use this series

This series has 4 levels. The facing page shows what you can expect to find in the books at each level.

As your child's confidence grows, they can progress to books from the higher levels. These will keep them engaged and encourage new reading skills.

The levels are only meant as guides; together, you and your child can pick the book that will be just right.

Here are some handy tips for helping children who are ready for reading!

 Give them choice – Letting children pick a book (from the level that's right for them) makes them feel involved.

 Talk about it – Discussing the story and the pictures helps children engage with the book.

 Read it again – Repetition of favourite stories reinforces learning.

 Cheer them on! – Praise and encouragement builds a child's confidence and the belief in their growing ability.

LEVEL 1 For first readers

* short, straightforward sentences
* basic, fun vocabulary
* simple, easy-to-follow stories of up to 100 words
* large print and easy-to-read design

LEVEL 2 For developing readers

* longer sentences
* simple vocabulary, introducing new words
* longer stories of up to 200 words
* bold design, to capture readers' interest

LEVEL 3 For more confident readers

* longer sentences with varied structure
* wider vocabulary
* high-interest stories of up to 300 words
* smaller print for experienced readers

LEVEL 4 For able readers

* longer sentences with complex structure
* rich, exciting vocabulary
* complex stories of up to 400 words
* emphasis on text more than illustrations

Make Reading Fun!

Once you have read the story, you will find some amazing activities at the back of the book! There are Excellent Exercises for you to complete, plus a super Picture Dictionary.

But first it is time for the story . . .

Ready?

Steady?

Let's read!

Michael Catchpool   Vanessa Cabban

WHERE THERE'S A BEAR, THERE'S TROUBLE!

LITTLE TIGER
LONDON

One brown bear saw
one yellow bee.
One yellow bee saw
one brown bear.

One brown bear thought,
"Where there's a bee, there
must be honey. I'll follow
this bee as quietly as can be."

One yellow bee thought, "Where there's a bear, there must be trouble. I'll buzz off home as quietly as can be."

Buzz! Growl! Growl! Shhh!

Two greedy geese spotted one
brown bear. They thought,
"Where there's a bear, there
must be berries."

So two greedy geese
followed one brown bear.
And one brown bear followed
one yellow bee.

Buzz! Growl! Cackle! Shhh!

Three shy mice saw two greedy geese. "Aha!" they thought. "Where there are geese, there must be corn."

So three shy mice followed two greedy geese. Two greedy geese followed one brown bear. One brown bear followed one yellow bee, who flew right into its nest . . .

Buzz! Growl! Cackle! Squeak! Shhh!

. . . and a thousand bees flew out!

"Where there are bees, there must be trouble!" cried Bear. "I'll run back home as quickly as can be."

"Help!" cried the geese. "The bear
is after us!"

"Help!" cried the mice. "The geese are after us!"

Growl! Ouch!

Squawk! Hiss!

Squeak! Eek!

BOUNCE . . .

WOBBLE . . .

One bear fell over two geese.
Two geese fell over three mice.
One yellow bee thought,
"I knew there would be trouble!"

CRASH!

Excellent Exercises

**Have you read the story? Well done!
Now it is time for more fun!**

Here are some questions about the story. Ask an adult to listen to your answers, and help if you get stuck.

Bear Hunt

In this story, the bear follows the bee, the geese follow the bear and the mice follow the geese. Have *you* ever played a game like that? What was it called?

Buzzy Bees

Can you count all the bees in this picture?

In a Flap

Now describe what is happening in this picture.

Happy Hobby

At the start of the story, the bear decides to follow the bee. Can you remember why?

Picture Dictionary

Can you read all of these words from the story?

bear

bee

brown

fell

geese

mice

one

three

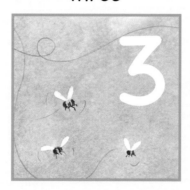

two

yellow

Can you think of any other words that describe these pictures – for example, what colours can you see? Why not try to spell some of these words? Ask an adult to help!

More Fun in Level 2!

Hopping Mad!

Fred has five frogs. Finn has five frogs, too. And when ten frogs get together, it is party time! But Fred and Finn do not find the froggy madness very funny . . .

Newton

Newton keeps hearing funny noises! "Don't be scared!" he tells his toys. And he sets off in the dark to find out what is making the scary sounds.

Ouch!

Hedgehog is about to go to sleep when OUCH! an apple lands on her back! Will her friends be able to help her?

The Wish Cat

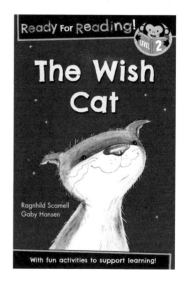

Holly wants a cute little kitten more than anything else in the world. But when she wishes on a star, she ends up with a scruffy cat instead!

For Mum — M C
For Cassie — V C

LITTLE TIGER PRESS LTD,
an imprint of the Little Tiger Group
1 The Coda Centre, 189 Munster Road, London SW6 6AW
First published in Great Britain 2002
This edition published 2017
Text copyright © Michael Catchpool 2002, 2013
Illustrations copyright © Vanessa Cabban 2002, 2013
Printed in China
978-1-84869-737-9
LTP/1800/1856/0417
2 4 6 8 10 9 7 5 3 1

More books from Little Tiger Press!

LEVEL 1 - For first readers

Can't You Sleep, Dotty?

Fred

My Turn!

Rosie's Special Surprise

What Bear Likes Best!

LEVEL 2 - For developing readers

Hopping Mad!

Newton

Ouch!

Where There's a Bear, There's Trouble!

The Wish Cat

LEVEL 3 - For more confident readers

Lazy Ozzie

Little Mouse and the Big Red Apple

Nobody Laughs at a Lion!

Ridiculous!

Who's Been Eating My Porridge?

LEVEL 4 - For able readers

The Biggest Baddest Wolf

Meggie Moon

Mouse, Mole and the Falling Star

The Nutty Nut Chase

Robot Dog